Positively Pets

Caring for Your Gerbil

by Kathy Feeney

Consultant:
Jennifer Zablotny, DVM
Member, American Veterinary Medical Association

Mankato, Minnesota

First Facts is published by Capstone Press,
151 Good Counsel Drive, P.O. Box 669, Mankato, Minnesota 56002.
www.capstonepress.com

Printed in the United States of America, North Mankato, MN.

Library of Congress Cataloging-in-Publication Data
Feeney, Kathy, 1954–
Caring for your gerbil/by Kathy Feeney.
p. cm. — (First facts. Positively pets)
Summary: "Describes caring for a gerbil, including supplies needed, feeding, cleaning, health, safety, and aging" — Provided by publisher.
Includes bibliographical references and index.
ISBN-13: 978-1-4296-1254-8 (hardcover)
ISBN-10: 1-4296-1254-1 (hardcover)
1. Gerbils as pets — Juvenile literature. I. Title. II. Series.
SF459.G4F44 2008
636.935'83 — dc22 2007030370

Editorial Credits
Gillia Olson, editor; Bobbi J. Wyss, set designer; Kyle Grenz, book designer; Sandra D'Antonio, illustrator; Kelly Garvin, photo researcher/photo stylist

Photo Credits
All photos by Capstone Press/Karon Dubke, except page 20, fotolia/Sahara Nature

Capstone Press thanks Pet Expo in Mankato, Minnesota, for assistance with photo shoots for this book.

092009
005604R

1 2 3 4 5 6 13 12 11 10 09 08

Table of Contents

Do You Want a Gerbil? 4
Supplies to Buy 6
At Home 9
Gerbils and Other Pets 10
Feeding Time 13
Cleaning 14
Gerbil Health 16
A Gerbil's Life 19

Wild Relatives! 20
Decode Your Gerbil's Behavior 21
Glossary 22
Read More 23
Internet Sites 23
Index 24

Do You Want a Gerbil?

Gerbils are small pets. They're soft and furry. Their tails end in bushy tips.

These tiny animals are very curious. They need a safe place to play, eat, and rest. A gerbil is a big **responsibility**. Is it the right pet for you?

Supplies to Buy

Pet stores sell gerbils and supplies. A cage or an **aquarium** makes a safe home. Gerbils also like a small, covered shelter in their home. They can rest inside it.

Gerbil food, a water bottle, toys, and **bedding** are other supplies you'll need. Don't buy cedar bedding. The dust can hurt your gerbil's lungs.

At Home

At home, you'll be excited to hold your new pet. Be patient. Talk to it softly, and let it sniff your hand. After a day or two, pick it up by cupping your hands underneath it.

Gerbils are wiggly. They can slip and fall out of your hands. Keep your pet safe by sitting on the floor when you hold it.

Gerbils and Other Pets

Gerbils like to be with other gerbils. It's best to have all male or all female gerbils. Males and females together may lead to unwanted baby gerbils.

Keep other pets, like dogs and cats, away from your gerbil. It's natural for dogs and cats to hunt and eat little animals like gerbils.

Feeding Time

Feed your gerbil once a day. Food made just for gerbils will keep your pet healthy. Gerbils can be fed anytime, but they mostly eat at night.

Always have fresh water in your gerbil's bottle. Clean the bottle at least once a week.

Small snacks can be good for me. Broccoli, apples, bananas, and carrots are some of my favorite treats.

Cleaning

Your gerbil stays clean by licking its fur. No baths are needed.

But you must clean your pet's home each week. First, dump out the old bedding. Then use warm, soapy water to wash your gerbil's cage. Dry the cage and add new bedding.

A clean home keeps me healthy. Don't wait for my bedding to stink up the room before you change it.

Gerbil Health

Healthy gerbils need **exercise**. They love to run in wheels. Put tunnels in the cage for your pet to explore.

If a gerbil stops playing or eating, it may be sick. A **veterinarian** can help. A vet should also see your gerbil once a year for a checkup.

A Gerbil's Life

Gerbils usually live from three to five years. As they grow older, gerbils eat less. They are less active. You can give your gerbil a healthy life. Give it good food, a clean home, and plenty of exercise.

My teeth grow all my life. Give me wooden chew toys to help me keep them at the right length.

Wild Relatives!

You may see your gerbil digging in its bedding. Wild gerbils dig tunnels in the ground. They use these tunnels as their home. When your gerbil digs, it is not trying to escape. Your pet is only doing what comes naturally.

Decode Your Gerbil's Behavior

- When they sense danger, gerbils make thumping noises by pounding their back feet together on the floor.

- Gerbils rub their stomachs against things to mark items as theirs.

- Curious gerbils sit up straight. They sniff the air while moving their heads and whiskers. When scared, gerbils become stiff and clench their paws.

- Gerbils wink their eyes when they eat something that tastes good.

Glossary

aquarium (uh-KWAIR-ee-uhm) — a glass tank where pets, including gerbils, hamsters, and fish, are kept.

bedding (BED-ing) — material used to make a bed; gerbils use wood shavings or shredded paper for bedding.

exercise (EK-sur-size) — a physical activity done to stay healthy and fit

responsibility (ri-spon-suh-BIL-uh-tee) — a duty or a job

veterinarian (vet-ur-uh-NER-ee-uhn) — a doctor who treats sick or injured animals; veterinarians also help animals stay healthy.

Read More

Koopmans, Carol. *Caring for Your Gerbil.* Caring for Your Pet. New York: Weigl, 2007.

Landau, Elaine. *Your Pet Gerbil.* A True Book. New York: Children's Press, 2007.

Petty, Kate. *Gerbil.* My Pet. North Mankato, Minn.: Stargazer Books, 2005.

Internet Sites

FactHound offers a safe, fun way to find Internet sites related to this book. All of the sites on FactHound have been researched by our staff.

Here's how:

1. Visit *www.facthound.com*
2. Choose your grade level.
3. Type in this book ID **1429612541** for age-appropriate sites. You may also browse subjects by clicking on letters, or by clicking on pictures and words.
4. Click on the **Fetch It** button.

FactHound will fetch the best sites for you!

Index

aquarium, 6, 14

bedding, 7, 14, 20
behavior, 17, 21

cage, 6, 14
cleaning, 13, 14, 19

digging, 20

exercise, 16, 19

food, 7, 13, 19

holding, 9

life span, 19

other pets, 10–11

picking up, 9
playing, 4, 17

resting, 6

safety, 4, 6, 9, 11
shelter, 6
sickness, 17
snacks, 13
supplies, 6–7

tails, 4
teeth, 19
toys, 7, 19
tunnels, 16

veterinarian, 17

water, 13
water bottle, 7, 13
wheels, 16
wild gerbils, 20